A Doctor For Abby

Jeanie Smith Cash

Copyright © 2012 Author Name
All rights reserved.
ISBN: 1495949508
ISBN-13: 9781495949500

DEDICATION

Dedication: To Jesus, my Lord and Savior, who made this all possible. To my own Granny Lottie who gave me the inspiration through the Lord to write this story. Thank you for loving me and for the light of Jesus that always shined through you. I miss you, but know that I will see you again at home one day. To my own special hero Andy, you are always there for me and I love you so much. To my sweet family for their love and support. As for God, His way is perfect; the word of the Lord is flawless. He is a shield for all who take refuge Him.
Psalms 18:30

Verse: "And we know all things work together for good to them that love God, to them who are called according to His purpose." Romans 8:28 KJV

CONTENTS

Chapter 1

Chapter 2

Chapter 3

Chapter 4

Chapter 5

Chapter 6

Chapter 7

Chapter 8

Chapter 9

Chapter 10

ACKNOWLEDGMENTS

I'd like to thank everyone who encouraged me to write this book.

CHAPTER ONE

Abigail Forrester ran through the airport pulling her luggage behind her. Thank goodness she had decided to fly out of San Francisco. The way she dodged in and out between passengers on the way to her gate, people would surely think she had to be crazy. But she had no choice. If anything held her up, she'd miss her flight. Her heart pounding, out of breath and with a pain in her side, she rushed into the security checkpoint and dumped everything onto the conveyer belt. She said a prayer of thanks when she slid through the doorway and didn't set off the alarm. After they finished checking her bags, she made a mad dash for the gate and arrived, as the agent was about to close the door.

"Please wait, that's my flight!" Abby handed him her ticket, hoping because she'd been upgraded to first class, he'd still allow her to board.

He frowned momentarily, but reached to accept the coupon.

"Follow me please. I'd suggest you give yourself a little more time in the future. Another second and you would have missed this flight."

"I know and I'm sorry. I really appreciate this, I was unavoidably detained." Heat filled Abby's cheeks as she remembered the reason she had been delayed. As manager of a travel agency in Tracy, California, a small town about fifty miles from the airport, she took pride in being organized. How could she have left her wallet locked in the drawer of her desk at work? She'd had to call Bonnie Cranston, owner of the agency, who had offered to bring the wallet to her. The hour and a half wait for Bonnie to arrive had almost caused her to miss her flight.

"I'll take those for you." The flight attendant lifted her bag and placed it into the compartment above her head as Abby took her seat and sighed in relief.

"You almost didn't make it." The man's deep voice echoed from the seat next to her.

Abby froze. She'd recognize that voice anywhere. Oh Lord, she prayed silently, let me be mistaken. Please don't let it be him. She slowly turned to look at the man beside her. She didn't know which one appeared more shocked.

"Nick?" She swallowed against a suddenly dry throat and forced her gaze to meet his. "What are you doing here?"

"I've been at a medical convention for the last two days." The dimples she remembered so well, creased his lean cheeks as he smiled at her. "Do you live in San

Francisco?"

"N-No." She stammered and could have kicked herself for allowing him to still affect her this way. She fastened her safety belt, before answering hoping to get a grip on her emotions. "I live about fifty miles inland."

"Jared said you'd moved away but he didn't say where." Nick placed the magazine he'd been reading back into the seat in front of him and adjusted his medical bag to give her more room.

Oh Lord, I know You have a reason for everything. But of all the people to find in the seat next to me, why did it have to be Nicholas Creighton? He hadn't changed at all. His muscular six four frame didn't sport an ounce of fat. Eyes a brilliant shade of green, dark brown hair that barely brushed his collar and a warm, welcoming smile that still had the power to turn her bones to liquid. How could she be so attracted to him when he'd crushed her the way he had? Even now, hurt nearly overwhelmed her at just seeing him again. The chance that she might run into him once she arrived at Granny's house had crossed her mind. But she hadn't been prepared for it to be this soon.

Nick and her oldest brother Jared had been best friends when they were growing up and they had gone to medical school together. Nick specialized in surgery and her brother Jared was a pediatrician.

"How's Janine doing?" She nearly choked just saying that name. She had spent hours on her knees the night Nick had told her he was going to marry Janine, asking the Lord to please make the other woman go away and that Nick would change his mind and come back to her. But that had been fourteen months ago. She hoped she'd gained some logic, since then, but considering her reaction to his unexpected presence, it didn't look hopeful.

The flash of pain that appeared momentarily in Nick's eyes before he answered, made her wonder if they might be having problems. "I'm sorry, maybe I shouldn't have asked."

"No, it's all right." He said softly and patted her hand. "You don't know do you?"

"Know what?" She asked as a slight frown furrowed her forehead.

"Nick took a deep breath before

answering her. "Janine died six months ago."

Abby gasped at his words. "I'm so sorry. I had no idea. My family didn't say a word." *Oh Lord, when I asked You to make her go away, I didn't mean for her to die! I just meant for her to move somewhere away from Nick, I didn't want her to have him. I was jealous, but I never meant for anything to happen to her.*

Nick interrupted her thoughts. "It's okay, Abby. I'm sure they were trying to protect you. I didn't exactly make points with your family after hurting you the way I did." He glanced over at her and she could see the regret he felt reflected in his eyes.

"Jared wouldn't tell me where you were when I asked, not that I blame him." His gaze slowly scanned her face. "If you were my sister I'd probably react the same way. He said he loved me like a brother, but you had made a new life for yourself and he felt it was best if I stayed away from you."

An odd mixture of emotions gripped Abby, sadness filled her heart at his loss, but she wasn't ready to forgive the hurt he'd inflicted. Still her conscience rebelled at the way she had prayed, it wasn't okay. Ashamed, she realized she hadn't acted with a very Christian attitude. Please forgive me Lord. Suddenly it dawned on her what Nick had just said. She sat up in her seat and looked at him. "You asked about me?"

"Yes." He smiled sadly, adjusting his medical bag under the seat in front of him to make more room for his feet. "After Janine died, I wanted to try to reach you to explain. I know I hurt you terribly but there is an explanation that I couldn't give you until now."

His hopeful look almost swayed her as she looked into his too-familiar eyes and felt a stab of long lost love. But at the last second, she came to her senses pulling her gaze from his as she reached up to turn off her air vent. "You don't owe me an explanation Nick. What we had was in the past. We've both made a separate life for ourselves now."

The captain's voice came over the intercom, interrupting their conversation. "Please fasten your seat belts and prepare for take off."

The plane taxied to the end of the runway. As they began their ascent, fear swelled in Abby's chest stealing her breath away and leaving her light headed. She gripped the side of the seat until her knuckles turned white.

"Still don't like to fly I see." Nick patted her hand gently. "It'll be all right."

Once the plane ascended into the air and leveled out, Abby released her death grip on the chair arm and her heartbeat slowed down to almost normal. She knew it was crazy to be in the travel profession and be afraid to fly, but she hadn't been able to get past the fear that always welled up inside of her. Just the thought of being so high off the ground caused her to break out in a cold sweat.

"Going home to Granny and Granddad Forester's for the

traditional Christmas Eve gathering I presume," Nick relaxed in his seat and offered her a gentle smile.

"Yes, I look forward to it every year. Besides, Granny and Granddaddy would be heartbroken if any of us were missing." She glanced away trying to fill her thoughts with her grandparent's and home, rather than the hurtful memories that the man sitting beside her brought to mind.

"Yes, they would. Jared and Amy invited Scotty and me to come for Christmas Eve. I hope it won't make you uncomfortable, they didn't want us to be alone."

Panic gripped her at the thought of spending more time in Nick's presence. How would she manage this? She had only been with him for a few minutes and already the painful memories flooded her mind. It wouldn't be easy, but she couldn't deprive him from being with his sister for the holidays. She adjusted her seatbelt to give her a moment to compose herself before answering him. "I can understand Amy wanting you to be there. You should be with your sister on Christmas Eve. Who's Scotty?"

"My son."

Shock rendered her speechless for a moment. Nick and Janine had a son together? Her chest tightened as she fought to control emotions she'd thought she had put behind her. *Please Lord help me, I need to get over this, or it's going to be a very long week.*

"I . . . didn't know you had a son." She stammered avoiding eye contact. "How old is he?"

"Six months and he's quite a little guy."

"Six months." Abby looked up at him. "Did Janine die in child birth?" Abby couldn't believe she'd just asked that. She been so shocked she'd just blurted out the first words that had come to mind. Her gaze searched his face, hoping she hadn't inflicted more pain with her thoughtless question.

"Yes," Nick said just as the pilot announced they were descending into the Denver airport. He smiled in her direction as if to let her know, he knew she hadn't meant to be unkind.

"I'm afraid I have some bad news, folks" The pilot announced just as they landed. "It's snowing so hard here in Denver they've grounded us for an indefinite time.

We aren't going to be flying tonight and they can't promise anything for tomorrow.

"Oh, no!" Abby jerked upright in her seat. "I can't stay here for two days. I won't make it to Granny and Granddaddy's in time to decorate the tree."

"I don't think we have much choice" Nick laid a hand on her arm in an effort to calm her. "They can't fly in these conditions."

"I have a choice." Abby pulled her tingling arm out from under his warm hand. She unfastened the seat belt and took her bag from the flight attendant.

"Abby, what are you planning to do?" Nick unfastened his own belt and it clanked against the airplane wall.

His shoulder brushed hers as he

stood up. It was times like this that Abby wished airplanes were larger. "I'm going to rent a car and drive." She slipped the strap over her shoulder adjusting it to a more comfortable position, as Nick reached under the seat for his medical bag.

He leaned over and said softly in her ear. "You can't drive thirteen hours in this snowstorm."

She moved her head as his warm breath tickled her ear, to avoid the intimate feeling it evoked. "Oh, yes, I can." Abby said a silent prayer of thanks, as the wall of people started moving toward the front of the plane. She followed trying to put as much distance as she could between herself and Nick. Just as soon as there was an opening, she quickly headed out the door and up the long ramp.

"Abby wait!" Nick called as he grabbed his garment bag from the compartment overhead and followed her. "There's no way you're going to drive that far in this weather by yourself."

CHAPTER TWO

A line had already formed at the Alamo Rental Car desk by the time Abby stepped up to wait her turn. She set her bag down and turned to face Nick as he came up behind her.

"Don't try to talk me out of renting a car. Whatever I have to do, I'm going to be at Granny and Granddaddy's for Christmas Eve." She raised her chin stubbornly, crossing her arms in front of her.

Nick smiled shaking his head and reached into his pocket for his wallet. "I'm not going to try to talk you out of it. I'm going to go with you."

Abby's heart did a little flip at the thought of spending thirteen hours in the car with Nick. Certainly a change from what she'd been feeling a short time ago on the plane. She'd only been with him an hour and a half and the wall of protection she'd managed to build had already begun to crumble. She couldn't let that happen. The guy broke her heart fourteen months ago.

Abby knew in her mind that she should detest him, but her heart wasn't listening. She had to get a grip on her feelings. She could not allow herself to get involved with him again.

Abby thought for a minute before answering, but she couldn't come up with an excuse that would make sense. "All right, we're going to the same place, so I guess it would be foolish to rent two cars. We can split the cost."

"That's fine with me." Nick pulled his credit card out of his wallet.

The tall dark headed man behind the counter motioned them forward. "How can I help you?"

"We'd like to rent a four wheel drive, please," Abby sat her purse on the counter.

The man tapped a few keys on the computer. "We have a Chevy Trail Blazer available."

Abby glanced at Nick and he nodded. "That's fine, we'll take it."

"I need the name, driver's license, and credit card of the person who will be driving." The clerk laid the contract on the counter.

"We'll both be driving," Abby said digging in her purse for her wallet.

"You'll have to put it in one name and then pay extra for the other driver."

"That's fine." Nick handed him his credit card and driver's license.

"Hey wait a minute," Abby protested as she continued to dig in her purse for her wallet. "I planned to put it in my name with you as the extra driver."

"Abby, it's going to be a long trip," Nick said. "What difference does it make whose name it's in?"

She started to argue but she hesitated when she heard the fatigue in his voice. He had been in a conference for the last two days. He was tired and yet he'd agreed to drive through with her in spite of that fact. "I guess it doesn't make any difference. But I'm paying my half."

"Fine we can settle up later. Let's just get this done so we can get on the road. It's going to take longer to drive than it would in normal weather, so the sooner we get started the better."

Nick's arm brushed Abby's as he reached for the pen sending chills of awareness up her spine. She stepped back away from him and waited while he signed the contract.

"Okay." Nick slid his credit card back into his wallet and grabbed his bags. "We're all set. Let's go get your luggage before we pick up the Blazer."

"This is it, I didn't check anything." She slid the bag back on her shoulder and picked up her purse.

His eyes widened "Where's your guitar? You never go anywhere without it."

"I don't play anymore." Nick's penetrating glance made her uncomfortable. She didn't want to discuss this.

"Why not?" He didn't budge waiting for an answer.

"I just don't. Look, it's not a big deal. As you said, we need to get the car so we can get going. We have a long trip ahead of us and right now I need to find a restroom before we go."

"The restrooms are right over there." Nick indicated the two doors down and across from them.

"I may be a little while. I need to call my parents and it should be a little quieter in there."

Nick nodded as he sat on a bench and laid his bags on the floor next to him. "No problem," he said, removing his cell phone from his pocket. "I'm going to call Maggie to let her know I've been delayed and see how Scotty is doing."

Abby left him there and walked to the door that said WOMEN. Tactfully ignoring a tearful young girl sitting alone on a bench, she walked to the other side of the expansive room and pulled out her cell phone. After a couple of rings her father answered.

"Hi, Daddy."

She heard the concern in her father's voice as he answered. "Hi, Sweetheart, are you all right? Where are you? Your mother and I were worried."

"I'm fine, but we're grounded in Denver and they don't know for how long. So we've rented an SUV and we're going to drive." She freshened her make up at the sink while she talked to her father.

"Abby, I don't think that's a good idea. You're going to be driving in snow and nasty weather all the way through, it's snowing here too."

"We'll be all right, Daddy. We have to get there so I can help Granny hang the ornaments on the tree and I'm not missing the

Christmas Eve gathering. This is the only way we can get there in time, but we'll be careful. I promise."

"You've said 'we' several times now. Surely you aren't traveling with someone you just met. I've taught you better than that."

The sternness in her father's voice brought a smile to her lips. "No, Daddy. I know him very well. Amazingly enough, Nick Creighton happened to be in San Francisco for a medical convention and we wound up on the same plane. He's driving through with me."

Her father's silence spoke volumes.

"Daddy, I know how you feel about the way Nick treated me, but that was a long time ago. We're just two people that need to get to the same place," Abby said as she placed her makeup back into her purse.

"You be careful. Remember how devastated you were the last time."

"I know, Daddy, but I'm not going to allow that to happen, so you don't need to worry."

"Well, I do worry. I like Nick. I always have, but after the way he hurt you, I don't want you involved with him." He paused. "I have to admit, though, being with Nick is preferable to you driving through alone."

Abby hung up the phone with a promise to call again soon and headed past the young girl who still sat in the same place on the bench. Something about her tugged on Abby's heartstrings and she hesitated.

Lord, if you want me to talk to

this girl. Please give me the words to say. Abby sat down on the bench beside the young woman.

"Hi. My name is Abby. Is there anything I can do to help?" The young girl glanced up and the desolation Abby saw in her expression, wrenched her own heart. The girl studied Abby for a moment and shook her head. "No one can help."

Abby laid her hand on the young girl's arm in a comforting manner. "Sometimes it helps to talk to someone. Why don't you start by telling me your name?"

The girl sobbed. "My name is Emily and I don't know what to do. I brought my boyfriend to the airport. I thought he just planned to go home to visit his parents. But before he boarded the plane, he told me he wouldn't be coming back." More tears rolled down her face.

"Well no wonder you're upset." Abby went to the sink and wet a paper towel. She returned and handed it to Sandy.

"I just found out a week ago that I'm six weeks pregnant." Her slender shoulders shook as she cried. "Can you believe he said he'd send me the money for an abortion, but he wouldn't marry me because he doesn't love me." She wiped her face with the towel Abby had given her.

How in the world did this little girl, get hooked up with the wrong guy at such a young age? She looked like she should still be home playing with paper dolls, not sitting in an airport bathroom pregnant and alone. *Lord, please comfort her.*

Emily folded the paper towel in her hand. "I could never destroy my baby. I already love it. I want to be a good mother but I'm scared." She looked up and her tear filled eyes begged Abby to understand.

"You love your child, Emily, so that's a step in the right direction," Abby patted her arm gently. "Do you have family that could help you?"

"I can't tell my family." Her eyes widened. "My father will be so angry he'll kick me out. He won't love me anymore if he knows what I've done."

Abby was appalled; she couldn't imagine a father that would kick out his child when she was in trouble. Her father would never abandon her no matter what the circumstances.

"Emily, I know someone who

loves you unconditionally. His name is Jesus and he loves you so much, he died on an old rugged cross to save you. He is the son of God." Abby squeezed her hand a smile on her face.

"You're a Christian?" She shifted on the bench until she faced Abby. "So is my grandmother. She asked me to go to church with her."

"Are you close to your grandmother?"

"Yes, I love Nana and I know she loves me, but my father wouldn't let me see her after my mother died four years ago. He doesn't believe in God." She fidgeted on the bench. "I hadn't seen Nana until I turned eighteen last month."

"That must have been hard on both of you."

"Yes, it has, I try to spend as much time as I can with her now. She told me that Jesus loves me too. But I've done things I shouldn't have and now I'm pregnant and I'm not married. Jesus probably won't love me now." She hung her head.

"Jesus still loves you and He is willing to forgive you, no matter what you've done. That's what I meant when I said His love is unconditional."

Her eyes brightened as she looked up at Abby. "Do you think He might forgive me then?"

"I know He will." Abby smiled. "He loves us so much He is willing to forgive us no matter what we've done."

"I'll have to really think about what you've said." Emily picked up her purse from the bench beside her. "Maybe I'll go and talk with my grandmother and tell her about the baby."

"She loves you, Emily. I'm sure she'll help you." Abby reached for a small tablet she always kept in her purse." Here are a couple of scriptures, I'd like for you to read." Abby wrote down First John 1:9, Romans 3:23, Romans 10:9, John 3:16, and Romans 10:10, then handed the paper to Emily along with her cell phone number. "I'll be happy to talk to you some more, or if you feel more comfortable, talk to your grandmother. But you need Jesus in your life. He will help you through this."

"Thank you." Emily stood and slipped on her coat.

"Will you be all right?" Abby asked as she slipped into her own jacket.

"Yes, I feel better now. I think I'll stay at Nana's tonight."

"That's a good idea. I'll be praying for you." Abby smiled. "Be very careful driving home."

"I will. I have a four wheel drive." She slipped the strap of her purse over her shoulder and started toward the door.

Abby followed her out. Before Emily left, she turned to Abby with a smile.

"I'm so thankful you came into the restroom today. I'll think about what you've said."

She left and Abby said a prayer for her. *Please Father, watch over her and her baby. Bring her to the saving knowledge of Your Son Jesus Christ. I pray her grandmother will welcome her and give her the help she needs. In Jesus name I pray, amen.*

Nick got up from the bench across from the restroom and walked toward her, carrying his bags. From the look on his face, she knew he wondered what had taken her so long.

"Why don't you let me carry that bag for you?"

Abby watched the young woman disappear into the crowd and smiled. "That's okay I can get it, you have enough to carry."

"Is that someone you know?" He asked and glanced toward the girl as she walked away.

"No, but she's upset and needed someone to talk to." Abby told him what had happened in the restroom as they walked across the airport.

"Nice guy." He shook his head. "I

hope her grandmother will help her, it's not easy raising a child alone."

Abby glanced over at him, realizing this would be something he would know in a personal way.

Chapter Three

Nick glanced up at the sky as they stood waiting for the shuttle. If the weather didn't let up, they were in for a miserable trip. He had to be crazy to let himself get caught in this situation, but he couldn't let Abby drive alone. He knew how stubborn she could be. She would go whether he went along or not. Besides, he owed her something for the way he had treated her fourteen months ago.

He breathed in the fragrance of her perfume, thinking how good it felt to have her sitting next to him again. She hadn't changed much in fourteen months. Five-four and slender built-- Her reddish gold hair still hung in curls nearly to her waist. He remembered how her bright blue eyes sparkled when she laughed.

He hoped someday she would let him explain why he broke their engagement to marry Janine and understand that, under the circumstances, he felt it had been his only option.

The driver pulled up next to the SUV and called Nick's name. "Be careful, it's really slick," Nick said as they stepped out of the van. Ice and snow covered the parking lot, and damp air hit them in the face, chilling them to the bone. Fortunately, he had ignored Abby's protest when they left the airport and held onto her arm, even though she insisted she could make it to the van on her own. She had slipped twice and would have fallen without his support.

"I'll walk you to the car before I get the bags." Nick smiled to himself when she didn't object. By the time Abby was seated, the driver had their luggage unloaded and Nick stowed them in the back of the SUV. She had just fastened her seat belt when he climbed in and started the engine.

******

Abby wanted to protest and insist that
she'd drive. After thinking about it, however, she decided being independent had its merits, but she knew her limitations and Nick had a lot more experience driving in this kind of weather.

"It'll only take a few minutes for the engine to warm up, and I'll turn on the heater," Nick said, rubbing his hands together to try to get warm.

"That would be good. I'm freezing." Abby's teeth were chattering.

Nick slipped off his coat and laid it over her legs. "That should help."

The jacket, still warm from his

body heat, felt good.

"But you'll be cold without it." She started to hand it back to him, but he laid his hand over hers. She jerked away as sparks of awareness shot up her arm at his touch. If he noticed her reaction he didn't respond to it.

"I'll be fine, this sweater is heavy." He turned on the defroster and cranked it up to the highest setting for her. "I'll change it to heat and defrost as soon as it gets warm," he said and pulled out of the parking lot.

Abby smoothed the coat over her knees. He was just as warm and devastating as she remembered, but what they'd had together must remain in the past. She'd made a new life for herself. A happy life. She had been happy, hadn't she? Of course she had.

They had been on the road for about two hours, and Abby realized she'd been dozing when Nick yelled, "Hang on!" jolting her awake as the car jerked to the right, the tires sliding over the ice-coated road. Nick fought the steering wheel, trying to avoid a head-on collision as another car spun into their lane. Abby screamed as the blazer bumped over the side of the embankment and slammed into the ditch. She jerked forward as her air bag went off. Her seat belt tightened, cutting into her waist and across her shoulder. Dazed and disoriented, for a moment her mind didn't register that Nick was calling her name.

"Abby--Abby! Are you all right?" She felt his hand against her face as he brushed her hair back.

"My cheek hurts." She touched her face and noticed a smear of blood on her hand.

Nick examined her cheek and reached into the back for his medical bag. He deftly opened a package of gauze, folded it into a square, placed it against the open wound, and taped it just below her temple.

"You have a cut here but I don't think it's deep enough to need sutures. That will hold it until we get somewhere we can do a better job." She squinted as he shined a pin light across the side of her face." The bright light against the darkness hurt her eyes.

"The air bag scratched your face and neck," Nick continued to check her for injuries. "Do you feel dizzy, nauseous, or hurt anywhere else?"

"I don't think so." She sat up suddenly and looked at him. "Are you all right?"

"I'm fine--just a little scratched up, too, from the air bag. But I'm thankful they went off." He set his medical bag back on the seat behind him. "We missed the other car. It spun out of control on the slick pavement. I need to go see about them. Stay here, and I'll be right back."

Nick returned in a few minutes and slid back into the car. "They must have been okay they're gone."

"Your quick reaction saved our lives." Abby thanked the Lord she hadn't been driving."

Shaken and still a little disoriented, she peered through the windshield. "It's really nasty out there."

"Yes, and it's getting worse by the minute." He placed his hand under her chin and gently turned her heard toward him, checking the bandage on her cheek. Evidently satisfied with the results, he turned the key in the ignition and started the engine. "We need to find a couple of rooms at a hotel and continue on in the morning. It isn't safe to drive anymore tonight. We were fortunate this time. I'm not going to take any more chances with you in the car."

Abby only hesitated for a minute; she knew Nick had a point. As much as she wanted to be home in time to hang the ornaments on the tree with Granny, she wanted them to get there safely. It had been a tradition, for as long as she could remember, for the boys to set up the tree with Granddaddy the day after Thanksgiving. They hung the lights and glass bulbs. Then on Christmas Eve morning, the girls had hot chocolate with Granny and hung the wooden ornaments. Abby looked forward to it every year.

"You're right." She drew in a shaky breath and picked up the contents of her purse from the floorboard where it had been dumped when they hit the ditch. "We don't want to have another accident."

"I'll do my best to get you there in time." She held the flashlight for Nick while he rolled the airbag up and taped it against the steering wheel, out of the way. "I know how important it is to you."

"I appreciate that." She moved

the flashlight over so he could see to roll and tape her air bag to the dash. "But as much as I want to be there, it's more important that we get there in one piece. Granny would have a fit, if she knew we were driving in this weather."

"Yes she would." He took the flashlight and laid it on the seat between them. She figured he wanted it to be handy in case they needed it again. "We need to get going, but we have a problem. Even if we can get out of this ditch, the snow is accumulating so fast on the windshield the wipers are having a difficult time keeping up. I doubt that we can see far enough ahead to find an off ramp. But we can't stay out in this for long we'll freeze."

Nick made several attempts to get out of the ditch, and Abby could sense his concern. Even with four-wheel drive, the tires couldn't seem to get traction. "Slide over here and guide the car. I'm going to try to push it as you give it gas and hope that will be enough." Nick slipped his coat on and went around to the back of the blazer.

Abby rolled the window down, but she could barely hear Nick with the noise from the wind and snow blowing into her face. He had to be freezing out there.

"Okay, hit the gas real easy." Nick yelled.

She pressed carefully on the gas pedal, and the car eased forward. It hit the pavement slipping and sliding on the ice, heading back toward the ditch. She couldn't see Nick. Panicked, she prayed he'd had time to move out of the way. Her nerves tightened and her palms began to sweat as she fought frantically to keep the car on the road. It bumped the edge of the ditch and spun in a circle before she could get it under control. Abby sat, shaking, with her head resting on the steering wheel, her heart in her throat. Nick opened the door and laid his hand on her shoulder. "Are you all right?"

Her heart thundered in her chest as she breathed a sigh of relief and thanked the Lord Nick was okay. "Other than being scared half out of my wits, I'm fine." She glanced up at him. "You're soaked." She slid over so he could get in.

"Just my coat. I'm dry underneath." He slipped his jacket off once he was in the car and tossed it into the back seat.

Abby fastened her seatbelt, and

Nick pulled back onto to the road. "We better start praying," he said. "We aren't going to be able to see to drive for very long in this."

"You drive and I'll pray." Abby bowed her head. "Lord, you know our situation here. Please send us some help. We need to find an exit and a hotel so we can get out of this weather. In Jesus name we ask, amen."

"Amen," Nick repeated.

A half hour later conditions had not improved. "Nick this is really scary. I know you can't see any better than I can. A lot of good it does to have a cell phone if it won't work when you need to call for help."

"I know. We must be in a dead zone." Nick cast a sideways glance at Abby and offered a reassuring smile. "There is no other option but to keep driving. Maybe a highway patrol car will come by before too long, to help us."

Fighting the urge to panic, Abby instead returned the smile. "I hope so, because if we run out of gas, we won't be able to keep the heater going, and without heat we'll freeze before morning."

"It'll be okay." He gave her arm a squeeze. "The Lord will take care of us."

Two hours had gone by. Abby glanced again at the fuel gauge. Every time she looked, it had dropped a little lower. If they didn't find help soon, they would run out of gas.

"There's a truck coming up behind us," Nick said. "When he passes us, I'm going to try stay behind him. That way I can follow his lights. He sits up high enough he can see better than we can.

Nick stayed behind the trucker for the next several miles. The snow accumulated so thick on the windshield the trucker's lights were all they could see. The gas gauge, now sitting on empty, made her more nervous by the minute.

"Look at that!" She could see his bright smile in the reflection from the map light he'd left on. "There must be an exit ahead. He's giving a signal."

"That's great." Her body tensed for a moment. She sure hoped he knew where he was going and he didn't lead them both into a ditch. They'd just have to trust the Lord in this one. "We can follow him off and find a hotel."

At the bottom of the ramp, a sign indicated Goodland, Kansas to the left. The truck driver went straight across. "Nick, he's our answer to prayer. Look, he led us off of the exit and then went back onto the freeway."

"You're right, Abby." This time Nick's smile was broad, warm, and genuine. "The Lord is faithful. It's amazing how much He loves us and that He always provides our needs."

Nick pulled into a parking space at the Howard Johnson Hotel. Abby scrambled out of the car, determined to pay for the rooms, since Nick paid for the rental car. As she started toward the lobby, her feet slipped on the icy pavement and she went down hard on her left knee. Before she could get up, Nick stooped down beside her.

"Are you hurt?" He wrapped his arm around her waist.

"I think I'm okay. I just skinned my knee a little." She winced as Nick helped her to her feet.

"Did you bring some snow boots?" She glanced down as he pointed at her feet. "I don't think those tennis shoes are good on ice."

She glanced over at his feet and realized he had on more suitable shoes with waffle- styles soles. No wonder he could get around better than she could.

"I think you've done more than skin your knee a little," Nick said as he looked down at her leg.

Abby realized he was right; blood had soaked through her jeans. Her knee throbbed and burned along with the abrasions on her face and neck from the air bag, but she didn't tell Nick that. He held her arm as he led her to the counter.

"We need two rooms," Nick said handing the clerk his credit card. "Non-smoking, please."

The clerk returned Nick's card and gave him the two room keys. The clerk glanced at Abby and back at Nick, noticing their injuries.

"Do you need a doctor?" He started to reach for the phone there on the counter.

"No, I am a doctor," Nick said as he slid his wallet back into his pocket. "But you do need to write up a report, because she fell in your driveway and injured her knee."

"I'll see to it right away," the clerk said, glancing at the hotel roster. "Dr. Creighton."

Nick helped Abby to the elevator and the bellhop followed with their luggage. Abby didn't argue because she didn't want to embarrass Nick in front of the clerk and the bellhop. But she would be taking care of her knee and other injuries herself.

Chapter Four

When Nick and Abby reached their rooms, the bellhop brought their luggage in behind them. He placed her bag next to the closet and took Nick's into the adjoining room. After he pocketed the tip

Nick handed him, he left, closing the door.

Nick pulled a folded blanket from the closet shelf and handed it to Abby. "Wrap this around you. You need to slip out of those jeans so I can see what you've done to your knee, and then I'll take care of the places on your cheek and neck. Do you have any others that need attention? "

"Just a few bruises from the seatbelt nothing that won't heal in time. I appreciate the offer, but I can take care of my knee and other injuries myself." The excitement of the day caught up with her suddenly and she slumped, exhausted, into one of the tan chairs that set across the room from the bed.

"Abby, I can see you're as tired

as I am. Let's get this done so we can both get some rest."

"You can go to your room anytime. I'm not stopping you. I can take care of myself." She insisted stubbornly. "I'm sure it's not that bad anyway."

"Let me be the judge of that. I'm the doctor here, and I'm not going anywhere until you let me see your knee." He stood there, clearly determined. "So the longer you resist, the less sleep we'll both get, and tomorrow is going to be another long day."

Abby sighed closing her eyes for a moment. She knew he meant what he said--if she didn't let him doctor her knee and other injuries, she'd never get to bed. She was just too tired to continue this argument.

"Fine!" She grabbed the blanket and stomped into the bathroom, shutting the door. When she pulled her jeans off and got a look at her knee, she sat down on the toilet lid as her stomach lurched. Her head swam, and she wasn't sure if she was going to be sick or faint. She felt like she might do both, so she sat there for a few minutes. When she came out a little later, she had the blanket wrapped securely around her and sat down in the chair. Her stomach felt even queasier, and she was still light headed. She had wrapped a hand towel around her leg. Her knee was a lot worse than she realized, and she had a huge bruise across her shoulder and her stomach from the seatbelt. That bit of information she'd keep to herself--as she'd told

Nick earlier, the bruises would heal in time. He didn't need to know exactly what bruises.

When Nick reached over to remove the towel, Abby said, "You better lay that under my foot, otherwise we'll get blood on the carpet."

******

Nick frowned when he looked at her knee. "You've really done some damage. Are you all right? You look a little pale."

"I'm fine."

Nick studied her for a moment. She didn't look fine. He'd bet she was nauseous and hoped she wouldn't faint on him. She'd never been very good with cuts of any kind and especially her own. "Sit still then while I get my bag. I'll be right back." He went into his room.

A minute later, he came back with his medical bag and knelt down in front of her, opened an antiseptic pad, and gently washed the area around the deep laceration.

"No matter what I do, it's going to hurt. I think the least intrusive would be to set you on the edge of the tub and wash it in warm water."

"Okay." She started to stand, but he lifted her before she could protest and carried her into the bathroom setting her on the edge of the tub. When he had her settled, he turned the water on and let it run until he had it adjusted to a comfortable temperature.

"I could have walked in here, you know." Abby looked up at him.

"I know, but this way we didn't drip on the carpet." It was also an excuse to hold her. He loved having her in his arms, even for a short time. "This is going to hurt. I'll do it as gently as I can. Are you ready?"

She took a deep breath and let it out slowly, then nodded. Nick gritted his teeth when she cried out as the water hit the open wound.

"I'm sorry honey. I wish there were another way, but it has to be done to keep it from getting infected." Tears rolled down her cheeks, but she didn't complain as he washed the wound with soap and water. He patted it dry, then covered it with an antibiotic ointment and bandaged it. Next, he took care of her cheek and the abrasions on her neck and hands.

"All done. Are you all right?" Nick asked gently, watching her while he waited for an answer.

"Yes. I appreciate you doing this for me." She smiled and dried her feet so she could step out of the tub.

Someone knocked on the door. "That will be room service. I ordered us sandwiches." Nick opened the door and stepped back so the young man could set the tray on the table. Nick gave him a tip, and he left.

"I wasn't sure I'd be able to eat anything, but my stomach feels a little better now, and I'm starving." Abby sat down across from him. They joined hands, and he blessed the food.

"We should try to get an early start. I'd like to leave around seven in the morning if that's all right with you?" He tore the paper from a straw and stuck the straw in his drink.

"That's fine. I'll be ready. I just hope the weather is better tomorrow." Abby sipped her root beer.

"I hope it is, too. But at least if it isn't, I'd much rather drive in the daylight." Nick finished his sandwich and leaned back in the chair.

"Even if we don't make it in time to hang the ornaments, I want you to know how much I appreciate you driving through with me, to try to get me there." Abby brushed the hair away from her face.

"I wanted to come with you and I'm going to do the best I can to get you to Granny and granddaddies on time. I know how important it is to you to be there." Nick looked at her and smiled.

They had finished eating, so she helped him pick up the papers from the food and tossed them into the wastebasket.

Nick went to his room and took a shower while he waited for Abby to get settled into bed. When he was through, he knocked on the adjoining door.

"Come in." She pulled the blankets up over her.

"Here's some ibuprofen, it'll help with the pain so you can rest." He handed her a glass of water and two tablets.

"Thank you." Abby took the water and swallowed the tablets.

"Sure, if you need anything, just knock on the door. I'll see you in the morning."

"Okay, goodnight." She slid down in the bed and closed her eyes just as he went into his room. He glanced back as he shut the door. She looked so beautiful--her image would stay with him the rest of the night.

Chapter Five

The next morning Abby had a hard time finding a pair of pants loose enough not to rub against her sore knee. After going through everything in her suitcase, she finally settled on a pair of black sweatpants. They would be comfortable since they would be riding in the car all day.

Nick knocked on the door adjoining their rooms.

"Come in. I'm almost ready," she said as he opened the door.

"How's the knee?" He sank his large frame into a chair across from her and placed the two cups he had in his hand on the small table beside him.

"Sore. I decided to wear my sweat pants. They won't rub it like my jeans would." She glanced over at him as she placed the last of her clothes in her suitcase and zipped it closed.

"I can imagine it is sore. Sweats are a good choice in this case." He smiled sympathetically. "I'll change the bandage when we stop for the night."

"I thought we'd make it home by tonight." She stopped what she was doing and looked at him.

"I don't think so. From the looks of the weather report, we'll have to take it slow. It's snowing too heavy out there for the plows to keep the roads cleared, and we'll be driving in this all the way. I don't want to take any chances, and as long as we make it in by tomorrow evening, you'll be there in time to hang the ornaments," Nick assured her. "Do you want to eat breakfast here or grab something at a fast-food on the way?"

"Are you hungry?" Abby asked. "If so, we can eat here."

"I have a cup of coffee, so I'm fine either way. I brought you a cup of hot chocolate." He handed her one of the cups he'd set on the table. "Be careful it's really hot."

"Thanks. With this I'll be fine for awhile, so we can wait and stop on the way." She reached for the chocolate and slid the lid open, blowing into to the top to cool it before taking a sip.

As they got into the Blazer, Abby noticed the dark clouds hovering overhead. The countryside was covered in thick layers of snow. It was still coming down steadily, and it didn't look like it would let up any time soon. Normally she loved the snow and enjoyed the beauty of it, but not when they had to be out driving in it.

She glanced at Nick beside her as he pulled out of the icy parking lot. His strong hands on the steering wheel expertly maneuvered the SUV on the slick road. She thanked the Lord that he had come with her--even though being this close to him rekindled feelings she had hoped were long gone. She knew there was a reason for them being on the same plane. She didn't believe in coincidence, the Lord had a reason for everything that happened.

Abby adjusted the blanket she had on her legs and moved her purse from her lap to the floorboard.

"Are you warm enough?" Nick started to reach to turn the heater up.

"Yes, I'm fine. The heat feels good."

Abby realized at that moment the reason she'd avoided dating the last fourteen months. She had declined every dinner invitation she'd received. She didn't have any interest in going out with anyone who had asked her. Now she knew why. She still had feelings for Nick. Sitting so close to him, she could smell the fresh scent of his cologne, a familiar fragrance, her favorite. Memories flooded into her thoughts of the happy times they'd spent together. She shook her head--time to get her mind back where it belonged. She couldn't afford to think about the past. It hurt too much.

"What do you do for a living in the little town fifty miles inland from San Francisco?" Nick asked. "Tell me about your job and where you live?"

This subject she felt safe discussing." I have a small one-bedroom apartment in a town called Tracy. I manage a travel agency in the mall there. My office is about two miles from my home, so I don't have very far to drive each day to get to work. I can park just outside the door, so I don't have to be out in the wind and weather when it's nasty out. "

"Manager, huh? Well, that doesn't surprise me, since you had your own agency back home. Do you like your job and living in Tracy?"

She knew what he wanted to know--if she was happy.

"Yes I do." She took a sip of her hot chocolate. "The owner of the agency only comes in occasionally.

She's good to me, and the agents I work with are nice people."

"Have you ever regretted giving up your agency and moving away from Pierce City?" Nick sipped his coffee.

"To be honest, I'd have to say yes. But I'm adjusting."

"I'm sorry Abby, for everything." His voice grew soft.

"Nick, that was a long time ago." She squirmed in the seat. "A subject better left alone."

******

Lord, I believe Abby is the mate you've chosen for me and you know how much I love her. Help me to be patient, to be able to win her trust and love once again. Please give me an opportunity to make things right between us. Nick prayed silently.

Just as he ended his prayer, he heard a loud pop, and the SUV began to swerve all over the road. He knew immediately they had blown a tire. He took his foot off of the gas but didn't hit the brakes, allowing the vehicle to slow down as he guided it to the side of the road.

Abby's blue eyes widened. "What happened?"

"We've blown a tire," Nick said and unfastened his seatbelt. "I hope and pray there's a spare in the back."

He climbed out of the car, and his boots sunk to his ankles in the deep snow. He shivered in spite of his heavy jacket. Wind and snow pelted him in the face as he made his way to the back of the Blazer. He opened the hatch to look for a

spare and jack to change the tire--
not his favorite thing to do in this
weather. It didn't look like he had
to worry about it, they didn't have a
jack. He closed the hatch and
climbed back inside. The warmth
from the heater felt wonderful as
he rubbed his hands together in an
attempt to get the feeling back into
his frozen fingers.

"We have a bit of a problem."
Nick sighed and laid his arm across
the steering wheel. "There's a
spare, but we don't have a jack."

"Great!" Abby turned toward him
in the seat. "Now what are we
going to do."

"I'll try my cell phone and call
AAA. Maybe we're in a place where
it will work this time." Nick pulled
his phone out of his pocket, flipped

it open, dialed, and waited while it rang.

Please Lord, I pray it will go through. We need some help here.

"It's ringing."

"Hello, AAA road service, how can I help you?" A lady's soft voice came through from the other end of the phone.

"We're on Highway 70 just a few miles from Russell, Kansas. We've blown a tire."

"Do you have a spare sir?" She asked.

"Yes, but we don't have a jack and we need some fuel. We're almost out of gas. We're in a light blue Chevy Blazer." He then gave her the license number shown on the rental agreement and estimated the closest mile post. Nick wasn't leaving it to chance that another

SUV would be mistaken for theirs.

"I'll send a rig out as soon as I can, but it may be a little awhile. We're swamped with calls. We have been all morning. There are a lot of people stuck in this weather."

"Okay. Thank you. I'm afraid we won't be going anywhere, so we'll be right here, when he's free," Nick said and closed his phone before slipping it back into his pocket.

"Well, that didn't sound too promising." Nick frowned. "I have a feeling we may be here awhile. They're very busy. She said she'd send a rig as soon as one became available."

Nick locked the doors and turned on the flashers. "I guess we might as well get as comfortable as we can." He slumped down and laid his head against the headrest on his seat.

"Abby, I'd like to explain to you why I broke our engagement." He closed his eyes and waited, hoping she'd agree to listen.

"Nick." She hesitated as if she were thinking about it, and his hopes rose, but in the next moment, she dashed them completely. "Please, let's not talk about that--not right now."

He sighed, gritting his teeth to hold back his disappointment. "All right, but one of these days we need to talk about it."

"Well, that may be, but please, not now."

He heard the crack in her voice. This was hard for her. He was to blame for that hurt, and his chest tightened with regret. Still he was frustrated at her continued refusal to listen to him. He hoped his explanation would make it a little easier for her. Maybe it would help to know that he had a good reason, as unfair as it was, for what he'd done. That is, if she'd ever allow him to give her his explanation.

Nick closed his eyes, and the memories of that night flooded his mind. Janine had come to him after his brother had been killed in Kuwait. She made him promise he would never reveal what she planned to tell him. After he gave his word, she told him about her pregnancy and that the child she carried belonged to his brother. She wanted to draw up a business arrangement with him. If he would marry her and give the baby his name, she would sign papers giving him sole custody, along with an annulment the day after his birth. If he wouldn't agree, she would have an abortion. He cringed even now at the thought of her destroying the baby.

Abby had shown such compassion to the young girl at the airport, and he loved her even more for it. He prayed she would allow him to explain and she would show him some of that compassion--and understand that he'd had no choice in the decision he'd made the night he'd broken their engagement.

Chapter Six

"It's been two hours since we called." Abby shivered and wrapped her coat more securely around her. "I wonder how much longer it'll be before they get here."

"I don't know, but surely it won't

be too much longer. I'll start the engine and turn the heater back on for a little while so you can get warm."

"I'm okay. I know we're low on gas and you're trying to conserve what we have. If we run out, we won't have any heat. I can wait a little longer."

"It won't take that much to run it for a few minutes. You're freezing, and I don't want you to get sick."

"Nick, I'm really sorry I got you into this. It was a foolish idea to try to drive in this weather. Now you're out here in the middle of nowhere, stuck, freezing in the snow, and it's all my fault. I didn't want to disappoint Granny and Granddaddy, but they wouldn't want us to risk our lives to get there."

"I came because I wanted to, Abby. I knew the risks. Besides, we're going to be fine. AAA will be here before long, and we'll soon be on our way again."

Abby sighed and leaned back against the seat. Nick had always been such a special person, and she could see that hadn't changed. She didn't know if she'd ever be able to trust him again, but during the time they'd been together on this trip, she had regained her respect for him. After all, he didn't have to come with her, and yet he hadn't hesitated, even with the severe weather conditions. He'd also done everything he could to help and protect her. She kept thinking about the situation they found themselves in. What if help didn't get here in time and this would be the last chance she had to find out what had caused Nick to break their engagement fourteen months ago and marry Janine? Maybe she should listen to his explanation. Otherwise she might not ever know.

She watched him for a moment. He looked so handsome, relaxed there next to her, his head resting on the seat. Just looking at him took her breath away. She still had feelings for him, but he had hurt her, and she was leery of him. Although, if she was honest with herself, she had to admit she was glad he came with her. Even though she wasn't ready to accept him back into her life, she didn't want him completely out of it either. Maybe what he was going to tell her would make a difference. She'd listen to him and then reevaluate the situation

"Nick." Abby said softly. "I've thought about what you said earlier, and I've decided, if you want to explain what happened fourteen months ago, I'm ready to listen."

He opened his eyes and scooted up in his seat as he turned toward her. She swallowed nervously. Had she made a mistake? Would what he had to say make things worse? Whether it did or not she had to know.

Abby sat quietly and listened as Nick explained exactly what had happened with Janine.

******

He flipped the map light on so he could see her face. The anguish he saw there and knowing he had caused it nearly ripped his heart out. Closing his eyes, he paused for a minute longer to regain his composure. He looked at her and said, "I couldn't let her destroy my brother's baby, Abby. Scotty is all I have left of Nathan. I didn't have any other choice. I just couldn't let her have an abortion. I'm sorry. If there had been any other way, believe me, I would have taken it. I never meant to hurt you."

Nick paused for a moment to give Abby time to take in all he'd just shared with her, praying she would understand and forgive him. He loved her so much. She was his life. He hoped they could still have a future together. When she didn't say anything, he continued.

"Abby, I felt terrible, and my heart ached and still does at the way I treated you. I had no choice but to break our engagement without giving you an explanation." At the sight of the tears welling in her eyes, he ran his hand through his hair and swallowed hard before continuing.

"I still have a difficult time understanding how my brother could have gotten himself into a situation like this. Nathan's Christian principles were as strong as mine are. But he loved Janine to distraction, and I have no doubt this child belongs to him." He paused and swallowed again. having a hard time keeping his own emotions under control while he finished what he had to say.

"I had no choice. I signed the necessary papers, agreeing to keep her secret until after the annulment and she'd left the area."

Abby glanced up at him as tears

spilled over and ran down her face. She impatiently wiped them away. Talking about this was hard for her. Nick knew her well enough to know that she would feel compassion for him even though she didn't want to. He'd hurt her that night, and she wasn't sure she could trust him. He couldn't blame her for not ever wanting to suffer like that again.

Nick saw tears well in her eyes again and felt like a heel, hoping as he finished his story she would understand and it would ease some of the pain and disappointment he knew she was feeling.

"There's something else that Janine failed to tell me--one very important factor," Nick continued as Abby reached into her purse for a tissue. "Janine had a severe heart condition, and the doctor advised against her carrying the child, explaining if she carried the baby to term, she'd never live through the strain of childbirth." He had to stop and clear his throat. His emotions were about to get the better of him in spite of his efforts to keep them under control. "

She left a letter with her lawyer to be given to me after her death. In the letter, Janine explained that she loved Nathan, and she wanted their baby to have a chance."

"If she loved him and the baby so much..." Abby paused for a moment and looked at him. "How could she even consider having an abortion?"

"I asked myself that same question. Looking back, I'm sure she wouldn't have had the abortion if I'd refused, but I didn't know her well enough to realize that. She probably felt that threatening to do so was the only way to guarantee that I would agree to her terms. She knew I would love and give her baby the home she wanted for him. In her letter she asked for my forgiveness for placing me in such a position. She just didn't know what else to do, she had to know her baby would be loved and cared for after her death." Nick shifted to a more comfortable position.

"In the letter she gave me permission to tell you the whole story." He didn't add that Janine's letter said she hoped that he and Abby would reconcile and raise the baby together. Nick would keep that part a secret for now and pray for Abby's love and understanding-- along with the right time to share that information with her.

"It was just a business arrangement Abby, we were never intimate. It wasn't a real marriage. I had an obligation to my brother's child, and I couldn't see any other way. I'd made a promise not to reveal Janine's secret before I realized what it would cost us. I never dreamed what she was about to tell me would change our plans."

She was quiet for so long Nick had decided she wasn't going to comment at all, but then she turned in the seat and faced him.

"I understand that you were faced with a difficult choice Nick, but still you devastated my world. I loved you so much--you were my whole life. I respect your having the courage to honor a promise, but we were engaged. You had an obligation to honor me, too, and I feel you owed me an honest explanation that night. What you did to me was unfair, and I'm sorry, but I don't trust you not to hurt me again."

"I'm sorry too, Abby. Not telling you what I was facing that night was a terrible mistake. I know that now, and I hope you know I would never hurt you intentionally. I love you. I've never stopped loving you. Can you honestly tell me that you no longer have any feelings for me? If you can truthfully tell me that, then I'll take you home and I won't bother you anymore."

Abby squirmed in the seat next to him. He prayed it was because she couldn't bring herself to sever their relationship completely and she'd admit that to him.

After a moment or two, she sighed. "I can't tell you that. I do still have feelings. But I'm not willing to pursue them right now. I need time to think and time to pray. I can't promise anything."

"I understand how you feel, and I'll give you all the time you need." As hard as it would be to wait, at least that gave him some hope.

Nick glanced up as lights reflected in the rear view mirror. "I think that's our tow truck. Stay inside here where it's warm." He grabbed his jacket from the back seat, opened the door, and stepped out as the large truck pulled up and parked in front of their SUV.

"I'm sure glad to see you." Nick walked up to him.

"Yeah ,it's a bit too chilly out

here to sit for very long. You have a spare?" The driver asked.

"Yes, but it's a rental, and we don't seem to have a jack." Nick opened the trunk and pulled out the spare tire. The tow truck driver took the tire, rolled it over to the flat, and proceeded to change it. Nick sure was glad this wasn't his line of work, and he felt for the young man having to be out in weather like this changing tires. But he was certainly thankful for his help. When the driver finished changing the tire, he added gas to the fuel tank. Nick gave him his AAA card, signed the necessary papers, and climbed back in the SUV with Abby.

"Man, it's cold out there. Even with my gloves on, my hands are frozen." He blew on his fingers to try to warm them and then started the engine. "We can use the heater again. He gave us enough gas to get us to the next town, which he said would take about a half hour from here."

With the snow coming down so hard, it was difficult to see very far ahead. Nick carefully maneuvered the Blazer onto the icy road. They certainly didn't want to wind up in another ditch.

This was crazy. Anyone with any sense wouldn't be out driving in this weather at all. But he'd do just about anything to make Abby happy, and he knew how important it was to her to be at Granny and Granddaddy's for the hanging of the ornaments and the family Christmas gathering. He'd pray for safety and do his very best to get her there on time and in one piece.

"That heat feels good." Nick kept one hand on the steering wheel and held the other in front of the vent to warm his fingers."

"Yes, it does. I'm freezing, and I haven't been out of the car. I can't even imagine how cold you are."

"I'm beginning to thaw out now. As long as I've known you, you've prayed for a white Christmas, I presume that hasn't changed." Nick grinned. "You sure got your wish this year."

Abby laughed. "No, it hasn't changed. I always pray for snow at Christmas. But I'm afraid I got more than I bargained for this time." As her laughter faded, she said, "I just hope it doesn't keep any of the family from making it this year."

"I wondered if you and your cousins would all make it this year since you all live so far away now. " Nick turned the steering wheel slightly when they began to slide a little on the slick icy road. He felt Abby stiffen next to him and then relax as the car stopped skidding before she answered him.

"It's been touch and go for awhile, but at least two of us will be there. Michelle is living in St. Louis, she's the closest to home. She's a kindergarten teacher there. She's bringing a friend named Matt Hall. Sandy called Granny and said she couldn't come, but I keep hoping she'll change her mind at the last minute and make it after all. You remember Jordan Fisher?"

"Sure, we went to school together." Nick corrected the car again and slowed down just a little. The roads were getting worse. He didn't know how much longer they would be able to continue to drive in this.

"He and Sandy spent time together when she was here visiting at Thanksgiving and they've been keeping in touch on the phone every since. When Granny called and told him Sandy wasn't coming home for Christmas, he decided to see if he could change her mind. I'm praying he'll be successful."

"I'm sure Granny and Granddaddy were pleased about that. Where is Sandy living now?"

"She lives in Little Rock, Arkansas and she's working for a veterinary clinic there. Granny and Granddaddy are thrilled that two of us are coming for sure. They're upset over Sandy and Nicole but they're praying and are hopeful they'll make it, even if it's at the last minute. Nicole called right after Sandy and said she couldn't come. She's living in Lexington, Kentucky. She works for a large florist. Part of her job is creating silk flower arrangements for the holidays and she feels she needs to be there for the Christmas open house. I keep praying something will change. If the reason she isn't coming has to do with someone special she wants to spend Christmas with, then I hope she'll decide to come and bring him with her." She grinned her eyes lighting with excitement. "It would be great if the four of us could be there after all."

"Yes, and if that happens, Granny and granddaddy will have a full house this year." Nick smiled. "I hope it works out. Everyone loves

Granny and Granddaddy, and it's hard to think of disappointing them."

"I know, I just can't imagine being anywhere else for Christmas. I've always been home with my family. I guess we're really fortunate." Abby opened a package of gum, offered him a piece and took one for herself before placing it back into her purse. "So many people don't have a family to be with."

Chapter Seven

Nick thought about the Christmases he had spent with his family. Now his brother was gone, and they would never have another Christmas with him. Yes, Abby was fortunate to have her family all together to celebrate with. He had to try to concentrate now on making new traditions with Scotty. He would be the best father he could possibly be and try to make Scotty's world as happy a place as he could for this little guy.

Nathan, I'll do the best I can to make your son a good home. I'll raise him to know the Lord, the way I know you would have, if you had been given the chance.

******

Abby glanced over at Nick. She hadn't thought about how he must feel. This would be a difficult Christmas for him and his family without his brother, and she knew how much Nick had loved him. They had been very close growing up, only eighteen months apart. He'd miss Nathan terribly. She remembered how hard it had been for Nick when Nathan told him he had enlisted and that he'd been deployed overseas. Nick had taken every extra shift available at the hospital to keep himself busy. She'd hardly seen him for weeks after Nathan left. Nick came to see her one evening, and apologized for neglecting her. He explained that he and Nathan had talked just before his brother shipped out. Nick told her that after spending a lot of time in prayer, he'd finally come to terms with his brother's decision. Even though it would be hard, he felt he could accept it. Then Nathan had been killed shortly after his deployment.

"Nick, I'm so sorry. I didn't think. I know it's hard for you this year. I'm glad you're both going to be with us for Christmas instead of being alone. By the way, where are your mother and dad?"

Mom and Dad are taking a cruise. They just couldn't handle being at home this year for the holidays. They needed something different. Since we lost Nathan in October, we didn't celebrate the holidays last year. And this will be the first Christmas since Janine's death, so it's been hard for them—for all of us--but having Scotty helps."

"I can certainly understand their feelings." She couldn't imagine losing either of her brothers.

"Abby." Nick interrupted her thoughts. "My parents don't know that Scotty isn't mine. No one does but you."

"Why?" Abby asked, confused

that Nick would keep this from his parents.

"I can see by the shocked look on your face you don't understand," Nick said.

"No, I don't understand." Abby looked over at him. "I would think it would be a joy to them to know they had a part of Nathan in his son."

"Janine didn't want anyone to think ill of Nathan, and she was afraid they would if they knew the truth about Scotty. You know how some people are in a small town. We love them all, but you always have a few that gossip every chance they get. Martha Ogalberry would have a field day with this. I can just see it. She'd tell Henrietta Stallings, and it would be all over the church in no time."

"Yes, you're right. I can understand her not wanting you to tell anyone else. But I know your parents would be thrilled to know they still have a part of your brother in his son."

"I'm sure they would, Abby, but I promised Janine I wouldn't tell anyone. The letter she left gave me permission to tell only you."

"Nick, I understand your loyalty to Janine. But I think under these circumstances, you need to think about what your brother would have wanted. You have to make a decision as to what is best here. She was trying to protect your brother's reputation, and I can relate to that, but maybe she didn't stop to think about how much it would mean to your mother and dad. They would really benefit from knowing you have Nathan's son. You don't have to tell anyone else, so that way you can still keep her secret." Abby thought about what she had said and wished she'd kept her mouth shut. She was no longer a part of Nick's life, she probably shouldn't have commented at all.

"Nick, I'm sorry. This isn't any of my business. Please just forget what I said and do what you think is best."

"If I hadn't wanted you involved, I wouldn't have told you any of this. I value your opinion, and you may be right, but I have to think about it and pray before I make a decision."

"I think that's a good idea to let the Lord guide you in this. That way you know you won't make the wrong choice."

A little while later, Abby was

getting hungry. With the time lost on the flat tire, they had missed breakfast, and it was now well past time for lunch. Her stomach growled audibly. Heat filled her cheeks in embarrassment, and she hoped Nick hadn't heard. But he chuckled.

"Obviously you're hungry. I think we need to find someplace to get you something to eat. It shouldn't be much farther to the exit. When we get into town, we can get some gas and find a restaurant. I'm getting hungry, too."

They took the next off ramp and pulled into a service station so Nick could fill the gas tank. Next door to the station, they found a small country restaurant. He parked the Blazer and shut off the engine. The cold wind whipped Abby's hair into her face as she stepped out of the car, causing her to shiver. She sniffed appreciatively upon entering the cheery dining area with its shiny white walls, red checked curtains, and tablecloths to match. Something smelled wonderful, and her stomach growled again.

Nick grinned as she felt the heat creep into her cheeks. "I'm sorry," She apologized.

"You're hungry, you can't help that." Nick pulled a chair out for her to sit down and then sank into the one across from her. On every table sat a candle, a vase with two poinsettias--one white, one red--with a sprig of Christmas greens in each. A red- and- green-checked bow decorated the vase.

Across the room sat a large stuffed Mr. and Mrs. Santa Claus in a rocking chair.

"Look at that, Nick. Aren't they cute?"

"Yes, they are. You obviously haven't lost your love for Santa." He chuckled.

Abby grinned. "No, I guess in that respect I'll always be a little girl at heart. I love Christmas."

Abby glanced around. In front of a large picture glass window stood a Christmas tree tall enough to reach the ceiling, decorated with red and green lights, bulbs, and lots of small wooden ornaments. It gave the room a festive glow.

The waitress came to the table, sat two glasses of water in front of them, and handed them each a menu. "Hi, welcome to Annie's Kitchen." She smiled brightly. "My name is Ellie, what can I get for you to drink today?"

"Root beer for me, please." Abby smiled and placed her purse on the chair next to her.

"I'll have a Dr. Pepper." Nick slipped out of his jacket and hung it on the back of his chair.

"I'll be back to take your orders in a few minutes." The waitress left to get their drinks while they looked at the menu.

Abby opened her napkin and spread it across her lap before she sat back to read her copy of the menu. "I think I'll have a cheese burger and fries."

"Sounds good. I'll have the same." Nick took her menu and set them on the edge of the table. When the waitress returned a few minutes later with their soft drinks, Nick gave her their orders. She took both menus and headed toward the kitchen.

"I told you all about my job and apartment in California." Abby reached for her glass of water and took a drink, more for something to do than because she was thirsty. "So now it's your turn. Are you still working at the hospital?" Nick's cologne wafted toward her. The familiar scent brought back memories of meals they had shared in the past, causing her heart to ache with what should have been as she waited for him to answer.

"No, I decided about six months ago to take my dad up on his offer and go into practice with him and your brother. There are four of us sharing the medical building now. Brad Collins joined our office. He specializes in Obstetrics and gynecology. He moved here from

Kansas City shortly after you left. He's a good doctor, one of the best in his field, and we were thankful to have him join us."

"That's great. And you're joining your dad should have made him happy. I know that's been his desire every since you started med school. It's convenient for the patience, too, to have a General practitioner, a pediatrician, an orthopedist, an OB/GYN all in one office."

"Yes, it's working out well, and I'm happy as I *can* be. But my life will never be completely happy without you." Nick looked directly at her, making her uncomfortable. She squirmed in her chair and quickly changed the subject.

"Do you have an apartment or a house?"

Nick sighed at her response and

took a sip of the water to wet his dry throat before he answered. "Janine had a rental, a two story house. I lived there until just recently. I occupied the upstairs, and she lived downstairs. Five months ago I bought forty acres and had a five-bedroom house built. It's a two-story with a full basement, and I had a barn with ten stalls built back behind the house for the horses." He smiled

"You have horses?" She cried softly. Riding Granny's horse Cody, out across her twenty-acre farm, was one of the things Abby missed.

"Six of them and two more on the way. It's between Pierce City and Wentworth. You'll have to come out and see it and the horses."

The waitress came back and placed their orders in front of them, along with bottles of ketchup and mustard. "Let me know if there is anything else I can get for you."

"Abby, is there anything else you want?" Nick looked over at her.

"No, thank you. This is fine." She smiled up at the waitress, and the girl nodded her head in response as she walked away.

"I'd love to see your place and the horses while I'm here." Abby smiled at Nick as she unwrapped her straw and put it in her root beer, trying to ignore the information about Janine and that she was ever a part of Nick's life. "Tell me about Scotty. What does he look like, and who keeps him when you're working?"

His eyes softened. "Scotty is the delight of my life. He looks just like Nathan. He hardly ever cries except when he's hungry, and he's been sleeping all night since he was six weeks old. I'm very fortunate. He's a good baby. I have a daytime housekeeper-nanny, Maggie Shepherd; she takes care of Scotty and keeps the house up."

"I know Maggie, she's a nice lady." Abby studied Nick as she ate her cheeseburger and fries. She could see the love in his eyes when he talked about the baby. Nick and Nathan had looked so much alike, people would never question whether Scotty was Nick's.

"Yes, Maggie's a special person. She's warm and loving, and she takes good care of Scotty. I don't have to worry about him when I'm away, like I have been the last two days for the convention and now our travel delay. Maggie loves him as if he were another one of her grandchildren. She's been keeping him since he was born, so he loves her too. I'm as comfortable leaving him with her for a few days, as I am leaving him with my mother."

"Have you thought about what you're going to tell him when he's old enough to understand? Are you going to tell him about your brother, or are you going to raise him as yours?"

"I've thought about it a lot. I'll probably tell him about Nathan, but we'll see when the time comes."

"If you do decide to tell him, have you thought about how your parents are going to feel when they realize you've kept this from them?"

Nick looked at her for a moment before he answered. "I've thought about that too, but I haven't come to a decision yet." He took the last bite of his cheeseburger and finished his Dr. Pepper.

Abby didn't say anymore. She just prayed he'd make the right decision. When he saw that she was finished, he reached for the bill. "I'll pay it." Abby grabbed for it, but Nick beat her to it.

"I've got it." Nick pulled out his wallet and headed to the counter.

Not wanting to make a scene, Abby didn't argue with him. She waited until they got into the car.

"Nick, I'm paying that bill," She insisted. "You paid for the food yesterday. It's my turn."

"We can settle up when we get to your Grandparent's okay?"

Abby hesitated. "All right, but only if you promise you'll let me pay half."

"Fine." Nick started the car and turned on the heater. "It's still snowing and getting deeper by the minute. I don't know how much longer we can drive in this."

"How far are we from Pierce City?" Abby wrapped the sweatshirt back around her legs.

"It's about six and a half hours. I hope the plows have been out on the highway."

Nick switched over to four-wheel drive and pulled out onto the road. "From the looks of the weather even if they have, they'll have a hard time keeping up, so I doubt we'll make it that soon."

Abby closed her eyes and laid her head back on the seat to rest for a few minutes. The next thing she knew, she'd been napping for three of the five hours they'd been on the road. She sat up and looked out the window, watching the snowflakes continue to drift over the countryside. The quiet seemed almost eerie. Nick reached over and turned on the radio, searching until he found a station playing soft music.

Abby appreciated the break in the silence until the song came on that had been playing the night Nick had asked her to marry him. The happiest night of her life--she had thought at the time. He had taken her out to dinner at a nice restaurant in Springfield. When they'd finished their meal, he had flipped open a small, black velvet box, and inside lay the most beautiful engagement ring she had ever seen. A solitaire diamond encircled with emeralds. She hadn't even hesitated when he'd asked her to marry him. She immediately said yes, beaming with excitement because she'd loved him more than anything. Everything had been wonderful in her world. Amazing how things can quickly change.

"Where are we?" she asked, her voice flat.

"Are you okay?" Nick glanced at her.

"Yes, I'm fine." But she wasn't. Tears filled her eyes, and she blinked rapidly to try to keep them from escaping and rolling down her face. She thought she had put this behind her, but obviously not, since just hearing that one song brought all of the hurt hurling back in one swoop.

"This is Vinita, Oklahoma. We're about an hour and a half from home. But in this weather it will probably take us a couple of hours to drive it." Nick leaned forward slightly. The snow had accumulated so thick on the windshield Abby knew he could hardly see through it. "A sign back there said there's a Holiday Inn Express & Suites at the next exit two miles ahead. I can't see a foot in front of me. I thought maybe we could make it on in tonight since we're close to home, but it isn't safe to drive any farther. We need to book two rooms for tonight and pray the weather will be better in the morning. Then we can drive on in tomorrow. If we get up early, we can still be at your grandparent's in time for you to hang the ornaments with Granny and the girls."

"I hope the other girls are there."

Abby worried about them, knowing they were traveling in this weather, too. The snow continued to fall, and there didn't seem to be any hope of it lifting anytime soon.

"I'll call my parents when we get settled in our rooms to see if they made it yet and let them know where we are. I'll be glad when we get there. It's almost as if we're out here alone with nowhere to go. It's a strange feeling. Are you sure we can make it another two miles in this?" Abby leaned forward and squinted to try see through the windshield better.

"Nick stop!" She cried."

Chapter Eight

Nick didn't dare slam on the breaks, so he tapped them several times, gradually bringing the SUV to a stop. They passed a car that had slid nose first into the ditch. Since the taillights were still on, the accident must have just happened. He pulled over to the side of the road, out of the way of any traffic that might be coming, and backed up carefully until they were just ahead of the car. "Stay here Abby." Nick slipped into his jacket. "I'll go see if anyone is injured and if there is anything I can do."

"I should go with you, you might
need some help." She started to unfasten her seat belt.
"There's no reason for you to get out in this weather unless it's necessary. I'll go check and let you know If I need, help, okay?"

"All right, I'll wait here. But please be careful."

Nick nodded and shut the door.

Wind and snow hit him square in the face, instantly chilling him to the bone. He slipped and slid all the way down the side of the ditch, sinking almost to his knees in the cold, wet snow making it difficult to move. Finally, he reached the door of the car. Concern filled him when he didn't see any attempt being made to get out of the ditch, or any movement at all. He knocked on the window; it seemed several minutes went by before it rolled down just a tiny crack. "Are you all right? I'm a doctor, is anyone hurt?"

"We're okay but the car is stuck," The man behind the wheel said. "We called AAA. They're sending a truck out, but the dispatcher said it would be about thirty minutes before it could get here. We appreciate you stopping. We have a full tank of gas, so we can run the heater. We'll be okay."

" I'm glad you're not hurt, Merry Christmas." Nick waved and headed back up the side of the bank to the SUV. He opened the door and climbed in beside Abby.

"Are you all right and is anyone hurt in the other car?" Abby handed him some tissues to wipe the snow off of his face.

"No, fortunately. They're just stuck. A tow truck is on its way." Nick slipped out of his wet jacket and laid it out in the back seat again to dry. There wasn't much he could do about his wet pants, but they'd be at the hotel soon. He started the engine and eased back onto the road. He'd be glad when they got to Abby's grandparents. This was the worst trip he'd ever made, and he wasn't looking forward to battling this storm the rest of the way home. Driving in this weather was just plain foolish. He'd much rather be sitting in front of a fire with Abby than out here on an icy highway. Of course, there was no way for him to know whether she would ever agree to sit by a fire with him again in the future. That thought didn't set well with him at all.

******

Abby stared out the window at the snow-covered countryside. Snow this time of year made it seem more like Christmas, but she didn't like driving in it. She watched Nick as he expertly maneuvered the SUV on the slick road. She had never met anyone that even held a candle to him, as the saying went. She realized, having spent all of this time in such close quarters with him, she loved him just as much as she had when he'd broken their engagement. She didn't want to love him, but she'd be lying to herself if she denied her feelings any longer. But was she ready to rekindle their relationship? She didn't know the answer to that question. She'd pray and ask the Lord to guide her and help her to make the right decision.

"There's the exit for the hotel." Nick flipped on the turn signal and took the off-ramp. "I'll be glad to get out of this weather and into dry clothes. I just hope it's better in the morning."

"I hope so, too." Abby unfastened her seatbelt as Nick parked in front of the hotel and turned off the engine. He came around and opened her door while she put on her jacket. She took the hand he offered to steady her on the slick pavement. She certainly didn't want another skinned knee.

The clerk signed them in and handed them their keys, and they went up to their appointed rooms. After the bellhop left, Nick knocked on Abby's door.

"Abby it's me," Nick said.

Abby went to open the door. "Come on in."

"Are you hungry?" Nick asked and reached for the room service menu.

"Yes, I'm starving. I hope they have something good in there."

"Well, let's take a look and see." He sat down beside her on the blue sofa and opened the menu, holding it where they could both read it.

"I think I'll have a turkey sandwich and chips," Abby said and leaned back against the sofa. "That will be fairly light. I don't want to eat something heavy and then go to bed on a really full stomach."

"Yeah, I agree. I think I'll order a club sandwich." He laid the menu on the dresser and reached for the phone. "Do you want milk or a soda?

"Milk please. If I drink a soda I'll be up all night." She sighed.

Nick dialed the room service number listed on a small card sitting next to the phone and ordered their supper. "She said it would be about twenty minutes. I think I'll go take a quick shower."

"I'm going to take one, too, and then call my parents to let them know where we are."

After Nick went to his room, Abby slipped out of her sweat pants. She covered her injured knee with a piece of plastic bag and the tape Nick gave her to keep it dry while she showered. The warm water felt so good. She didn't know when she'd been so tired. She washed her hair, then stepped out onto the small rug. After drying with the large, fluffy towel, she removed the tape and plastic bag from her knee and threw it in the trash. When she was finished, she dressed in a pair of green sweats and went out to call her parents.

Nick knocked on the door just as she hung up the phone. She opened it, and a young man followed Nick in with their orders and placed them on the table. He thanked Nick for the tip and left.

They sat down at the table, and Nick said a blessing. Abby opened the lids, and handed Nick his plate, and placed a napkin in her lap.

"I just talked with Maggie, and Scottie is doing great. I sure miss the little guy. "Did you get a chance to call your folks?" Nick asked.

"Yes, they were relieved to hear from me and know we're okay." She took a bite of her sandwich, chewed it, and swallowed. "Michelle and her friend Matt arrived safely last night. I'm so thankful to know they're all right. They haven't heard anymore from Sandy and Nicole."

"I'm sorry. I know you're disappointed. I'm glad Michelle and her friend made it okay, and I'll be glad when we get there, as well. Anything can happen in this kind of weather. It isn't safe to be traveling in it."

They finished their meal, and Nick helped Abby clean up the trash

"Let's change the bandage on your knee before I go to my room," Nick sat in a chair and opened his medical bag. Abby pulled the leg of her sweats up enough that he could remove the tape and gauze. She closed her eyes and braced herself, expecting the gauze to stick to the wound and pull the top off. When she didn't feel any pain, she opened her eyes, surprised to see the bandages already in the trash. Whatever Nick had used on her knee hadn't stuck to the bandage. Relieved, she leaned back and relaxed while he put on a new one. He smelled so good. Being here with him stirred her senses. His strong hands gentle as he worked on her knee. The touch of his fingers on her skin sent a tingle of awareness up her spine.

"It looks pretty good--no sign of infection," Nick said, jolting her from her thoughts as he put supplies back into his bag and closed the top.

She was thankful for the interruption. What was she doing? She couldn't allow herself to think like that.

"I called the desk and requested a wake-up call for five o'clock. That should give us plenty of time to get ready to leave and still make it your Grandparents in time for you to hang the ornaments." He cupped her chin in his hand and placed a kiss on her cheek. "Goodnight. I'll see you in the morning," he said and left, locking her door behind him.

Abby lay awake for a long time, thinking and praying. She knew there was a reason the Lord had brought her and Nick together. Was it in His plan for them to have a future? Could she put what happened with Janine in the past and give Nick another chance? She had been so jealous of Janine, but the thought of her dying so young disturbed Abby. She'd never wanted anything like this to happen. She couldn't help but feel bad. It had to have been hard for Janine to know she was dying and that she would have to leave her baby to be raised by someone else.

Abby's heart ached at the thought of what she must have gone through. Nick would be a good father to Scotty, but he also needed a mother. She sat up in the bed. Was this the Lord's plan? The reason He had brought them together. Did He want her and Nick to raise Scotty?

Chapter Nine

The next morning Nick knocked on Abby's door at five thirty. When she opened it, he handed her a cup of hot chocolate and a doughnut. "I thought this would tide us over until we get home."

"Thank you. I appreciate it." She smiled as he sat down across from her.

They quickly finished their breakfast and grabbed their luggage just as someone knocked on the door. Nick went to answer it. When he opened the door, the hotel manager was standing there.

"Dr. Creighton, I'm sorry to bother you, but there has been an accident. One of our guests just fell down the stairs. I called 911, but they said it will be awhile before they can get here."

Nick grabbed his bag and followed the man down the hall, with Abby close behind them. At the bottom of the staircase a man sat on the floor beside a young woman whose leg lay at an odd angle. They both appeared to be in their mid twenties. Even to Abby who'd never had any medical training; it was obvious the woman's leg was broken.

Nick stooped down next to her. "This is Abby, and I'm Dr. Creighton, looks like you took a pretty good fall."

She looked up at him. "This isn't a very nice way to end our honeymoon." Tears welled in her brown eyes. "I'm sorry Kevin."

"Honey, it was an accident, you don't have anything to be sorry for. Dr. Creighton, I didn't want to try to move her. She fell from about midway up the stairs. I'm Kevin Standridge and this is my wife, Cindy."

"That was a wise decision. It's nice to meet you both, but I wish it were under different circumstances.

Let's take a look at you, Cindy. Do you hurt anywhere besides your leg?"

"I hurt all over." She looked up at him. "But I think I'm just bruised. My leg is the only thing that really hurts. I'm sure it's broken."

"I could pretty well guess it is, but let's take a closer look. I'll try to be as gentle as I can."

When Nick touched her leg, she cried out. "I know that hurts. I'm sorry. It's definitely broken in at least two places. There isn't a lot I can do here. You need to go to the hospital to be x-rayed. Kevin, I don't want to move her. Nick turned to the hotel manager and asked if he could get them a pillow and a blanket. He returned with it and Kevin placed the pillow under Cindy's head while Nick covered her with the blanket.

"Hopefully that will make you a little more comfortable until the ambulance gets here." Nick smiled sympathetically.

Abby prayed for Cindy as she gasped in pain when she tried to shift into a more comfortable position on the floor. "Cindy, I know the floor isn't very comfortable, but it would be best if you try not to move until the ambulance gets here and they can get you to the hospital for x-rays." Nick advised.

From the looks of Cindy's leg, Abby knew she had to be in a lot of pain. In all of her twenty-two years, Abby had been fortunate never to have had a broken bone. Therefore, she didn't know from experience, but she could imagine how badly it had to hurt.

"Oh, I feel sick." Cindy placed her hand over her mouth as if she was going to vomit.

Abby ran to the counter. "Do you have anything she can use?"

The man at the counter handed her a plastic wastebasket. Abby ran back and handed it to Cindy, then went into the restroom and wet a couple of paper towels and took them to her.

"Thank you," she said just as she lost the contents of her stomach.

Kevin took the wet paper towels and bathed Cindy's face, all the while crooning lovingly to her.

"There's the ambulance," Nick said as sirens sounded from a distance. He explained Cindy's injury to the paramedics when they came in the door with a gurney.

Kevin shook Nick's hand." Thank

you, Dr. Creighton. We appreciate your help, and it was nice to meet you and Abby. I don't know how far you have to go, but it's nasty out there. We'll keep you in our prayers for a safe trip."

"I couldn't do much," Nick said. "But you'll be in our prayers as well. Cindy, I wish you the best."

"Thank you," Cindy said as the Paramedics wheeled her out the door with Kevin following.

"Well, we've had a pretty exciting morning. I sure hope Cindy will be all right." Abby picked up her purse and overnight bag from the floor next to the stairway.

"It will take some time, but I think she'll be okay. I hope her leg won't require surgery, I didn't feel any obvious splinters in the bone, but you never know for sure until you see the x-rays."

Nick was a good doctor. Abby was touched by his kind and caring attitude. "I'll keep them in my prayers. I'm glad she gave me her card with her email address. I gave her mine, and she said she'd send me a note to let us know how she's doing. I feel for them. Cindy said they'd only been married a week. Fortunately, she said their honeymoon was over they were leaving to go home. It would have been really awful if she had fallen on their first day." Abby glanced down at Cindy's business card. "Wow, it says here on her card she's a Christian Romance Author. They aren't very far from Pierce City. They live in Springfield. What a story for a new book huh?" She giggled as they went out the door and headed for the parking lot.

******

Nick chuckled. "Another author to add to your collection." He knew how she loved to read Christian romance. When they were together, she must have had more than a hundred books in her collection.

"Do you still have all of your books?" He asked as they climbed into the Blazer and closed the doors.

"Yes, I still have them and I've added a few since I saw you last." She grinned and reached to fasten her seatbelt. "I still collect my favorite authors. I went to the Christian section at the book store and bought their new ones before I left so I could bring them with me."

"You've read those same authors for a long time. I remember seeing their books on your shelves." Nick glanced over at her.

"Yes, I still have every book they've written in my bookcase at the apartment in California.

"Books and dolls--you always did love them." Nick smiled at her. "It's nice to have hobbies you enjoy.

******

Abby smiled to herself. Nick had always been tolerant of her love of books and dolls. Actually, he had always wanted her to have anything that made her happy. She knew that wasn't always true in every relationship. She had friends that weren't so fortunate. She had spent a long time in prayer last night before she went to sleep, asking the Lord to please help her to make the right decision about Nick, and she believed He'd given her an answer. He helped her to realize that Nick was everything she had ever wanted in a husband. She couldn't ask for a more dedicated Christian man, plus he shared her beliefs. After much soul searching, she decided she'd put her trust in Nick one more time.

"You're awfully quiet this morning. Are you okay?" Nick asked softly.

"Yes, I'm fine. I've just been thinking. I spent some time in prayer last night and I've made some decisions." She looked at him and tears filled her eyes. She blinked, and they spilled over, making a path to her chin. She wiped them away with the back of her hand. "I love you Nick."

He pulled the car over to the side of the road and parked. As he turned, he drew her into his arms. "I love you, too, Abby, with every part of me. You are my life. I haven't been whole since the night we parted. If you can find it in your heart to forgive me and give me another chance, I promise I won't ever hurt you again."

"Through long hours of prayer as I lay awake last night and with the Lord's help. I came to the realization that under the circumstances with Janine, you made the only choice you could have made."

******

Nick's heart sang with happiness. He'd waited so long for this day. *Thank you Lord*, he breathed silently as he kissed Abby, holding her close. He cupped her chin, gently lifting it where he could see her face. "I love you so much, Abby. I want to spend the rest of my life with you, doing everything I possibly can to make you happy. Would you be willing to move back to Pierce City? Will you marry me, be my wife, and a mother to Scotty?"

His chest tightened as he waited anxiously for her to answer.

"Yes, I'll move back to Pierce City. I haven't truly been happy since I left. Just being with you will make me happy." She ran her fingers through his hair. "And yes, I'll marry you. I look forward to being your wife, and I'll do my best to be a good mother to Scotty."

He breathed a sigh of relief and gently squeezed her hand. "I have your ring in my safe at the house. We can go by and get it on the way to Granny and Granddad's." He looked directly into her eyes for a moment. "Now I'd like to know why you won't play your guitar anymore."

She looked away. "Because it brought to mind too many hurtful memories. You loved to hear me play, and every time I picked up my guitar, I saw your face. The way you used to close your eyes and listen so intently when I'd play and sing--it broke my heart, so I put the guitar in Granny and granddad's bedroom closet and closed the door. It's still there."

"Abby, I'm so sorry." He placed a finger under her chin and turned her head toward him. "Will you play it again for me?"

She looked at him for a moment and then nodded.

"One more thing before we drive into town. You need to prepare yourself for what you're going to see. I know you saw all the coverage on the damage Pierce City suffered from the tornado. But watching it on television and seeing it in person is a totally different thing. The whole downtown was devastated. There wasn't much left standing. They're rebuilding, but it doesn't look anywhere near the same as it did when you left." Nick kissed her once more before he started the car and pulled back onto the highway.

Chapter Ten

They drove into Pierce City about an hour later. "Oh Nick!" Abby cried placing her hand over her mouth in shock. "I can't believe this. You weren't kidding when you said the tornado didn't leave much. It did so much of damage." The devastation was incredible. Sadness washed over her. There were a few of the original buildings still standing that had been repaired, but most of them were gone. She remembered the last Happy Neighbor Days gathering she had been to. She could close her eyes and picture it as it had been.

"It breaks my heart. Almost all of those quaint old buildings are gone now. But we're very fortunate there weren't more killed or injured and that's the most important thing. The Lord really protected our families. Fortunately they live three miles out in the country. They're far enough away from town that they weren't effected by the tornado, and for that I'm very thankful."

"I know, Sweetheart." Nick sighed. "I am, too, and as you can see, they're rebuilding the downtown area. It won't be long now. They're almost finished. The businesses will soon be back up and functioning again. It will never be quite the same, but as close as they can make it. The love and closeness of the people in this town can never be destroyed, and that's what matters."

Abby smiled sadly as they drove the rest of the way through town on their way to Nick's house. So many memories flashed through her mind. She had grown up in this quaint little town.

"You're right, and I'm thankful to see they're almost done. I love this town and all of the people in it. I always have. It will always be my home."

Nick stopped in front of a set of gates and unlocked the chain holding them closed, then slid the gate open and got back into the Blazer. A few minutes later, he parked in front of a large Victorian style house. She loved it. It was exactly what she would have built. It stood two stories tall with a wide front porch and surrounded by trees. A Large red barn almost as big as the house sat back and to the right side of the property. It was quite an impressive place. Since they were short on time Abby waited in the car while Nick went in to get her ring. But she intended to have a full tour of it when they had more time. Excitement at the thought of living in this beautiful place with Nick and Sctty made her giddy. She wanted to get out and do a little dance around the yard. She refrained herself but just barely. Wouldn't that be a sight? She laughed.

Nick placed some Christmas packages in the trunk and then slid in beside her a few minutes later and started the car. As they drove back down the long driveway, Abby glanced behind her.

"Is Scotty okay? I thought you'd bring him with you." She turned back around and refastened her seatbelt.

"He's fine. I planned to bring him, but he was asleep. When I stepped into his room Maggie was just laying him down. I thought about bringing him with us anyway, I really missed him, and if we didn't have a big night, I would have. But I don't want him to be cranky so I decided to let him take his nap. Maggie said she'd call me as soon as he wakes up and I'll come back and get him.

"I'm disappointed. I understand he needs his nap, but I can't wait to see him."

"I'm glad you feel that way." He took her hand in his and squeezed it gently. "When we get Christmas over with I'll bring you out and give you a tour of your new house." He grinned.

I love your house. I can't wait to see the inside. It's so beautiful out here with all of these trees. I'll bet it's gorgeous in the springtime when all of their branches are filled with lush green leaves."

"It's our house, and it is beautiful in the spring, that's one of the reasons I built out here in the country. It was with you in mind. I prayed every night that one day soon you'd share it with me." Nick glanced over at her, a smile creasing his handsome face. He stopped to lock the gate and then headed toward Pierce City, so the girls could have their traditional breakfast with Granny and hang the ornaments.

They drove up the long driveway, and just as they pulled up in front of Granny and Granddaddy Forrester's house, Abby's cell phone rang.

Abby slid her phone out of the case and answered. "Hello?"

"Hi Abby, this is Emily. Remember me? We met in the women's restroom at the airport."

"Emily, I'm so glad to hear from you. How are you?"

"I'm just fine. I've moved in with my grandmother now, and she is going to help me with the baby. I wanted to call and tell you that I read the scriptures you gave me. Between reading them and talking to my grandmother, I've asked Jesus to come into my heart."

"Emily, that's wonderful. I'm so

thrilled."

"I just want to thank you for caring enough to take the time for a lonely, devastated girl, you didn't even know. You are a special person, Abby. Because of you, I have found Jesus and He has changed my life. Have a very nice Christmas, and I'll be in touch again soon."

"That's great, Emily. I'm so happy for you. You have a Merry Christmas, too. I'll keep you in my prayers and look forward to hearing from you again." Abby hung up the phone and shared their conversation with Nick.

"That's fantastic, Sweetheart. You just never know where the Lord is going to give you an opportunity to witness for Him. We need to always be ready for any opportunity. He lies before us. A few short minutes in that airport bathroom and you led a lost soul to Jesus." He smiled and wrapped his arm around Abby's shoulders as they walked up the steps that led to the wide front porch. Before they went in the door, Nick drew Abby into his arms and kissed her. "Can we sit on the swing for a minute before we go inside?" Nick asked.

"Sure." Abby walked across the porch with him, and they sat on the swing. Nick reached for her left hand and slipped the engagement ring onto her finger. "Now it's back where it belongs." He smiled and kissed her forehead.

Thank you, Nick. I love this ring. I've missed it, and I've missed you." She leaned over and hugged him.

"I've missed you too, and I feel this is going to be our best Christmas ever. To start with, I'd like for you to open this gift before you go in. The others I put in the trunk. I'll give them to you tonight when we have the traditional gathering around the tree." Nick handed her a small brightly, wrapped package. Abby tore the paper and opened the box. "Oh, Nick!" She cried softly. "It's perfect. I love it." She grinned and lifted the Christmas ornament from the bed of cotton. "A wooden guitar. It looks exactly like mine." It had 'Branson' with last year's date painted on the front. She looked up at him, confused. "Why does it have last year's date instead of this year's?"

He smiled. "I bought it last year,

along with the others. We were separated shortly afterwards, and I never had an opportunity to give them to you. I kept them, praying I'd have another chance. I'm glad you like the ornament. I wanted you to have it to hang on the tree this morning."

"Thank you, Nick. I'll cherish it, and it will always be a special reminder, of just how blessed we are to have another chance to be together."

Nick drew her to him again and kissed her. She loved the secure feeling of being held in his strong arms. "Nick, what do you think about getting married on Valentine's Day?"

"Whatever makes you happy, Sweetheart, as long as it isn't too far away." He kissed her.

As they sat there for a few minutes in the quiet country atmosphere on her grandparent's porch before joining the family, Abby realized that the Lord had brought her and Nick back together to raise a beautiful little boy and He had brought them home safely in time to spend Christmas with her family. He used the situation for her to witness to a devastated young girl, bringing Emily into the family of God. The Lord certainly worked something good out of their suffering. Romans 8:28 came to mind. *'And we know all things work together for good to them that love God, to them who are called according to His purpose.'* Sitting there in Nick's arms, Abby prayed silently, thanking and praising the Lord for all of their blessings. She had made a Christmas wish, asking God to provide a way for her to be home for Christmas. Not only had He granted that request, but He had reunited her with Nick, her true love, her soul mate.

A Doctor for Abby
Epilogue

Nick glanced up and noticed Lottie Ann Forrester, Granny to all of her grandchildren. She stood at the top of the stairs next to Granddaddy Audrey, beaming with pride as they watched their family below. She spoke just loud enough for Nick to hear what she was saying to her husband as they descended the stairs together. "I love seeing all of our children and grandchildren gathered around my grand piano that has resided in that same corner of our home for so many years. It warms my heart to see Abigail sitting on the bench playing Christmas carols while the others sing along. I enjoy watching the Christmas tree lights as they twinkle reflecting on the wooden ornaments our four granddaughters have collected over the years.

"Yes. "Audrey glanced at his wife. "And it warms my heart to see you so happy."

Look Audrey, snow is falling outside the window. It's drifting onto the wooden corners of each pane of glass." She smiled at him. "Isn't it wonderful to hear the laughter as it fills our house once again and to listen to the girls as they share stories from their morning of hanging the ornaments?"

"Yes, I enjoy Christmas Eve more every year." Granddad agreed. "The Lord has blessed us, we have a loving family and every member has made it here, to be with us tonight." Granny held onto the banister as they made their way down the steps, to join in the fun. "I can remember our granddaughters and their antics as they were growing up, each one bring a smile to my face." She said as she glanced at her husband.

"Granny, Grandad are you okay?"

Nick stood waiting for them as they reached the bottom of the stairs.

"Yes, Darling, we're fine and I have a story to share with my future grandsons." Nick smiled as Granny grinned at her granddaughters when they saw them exchange a look that clearly said, you know it's something embarrassing.

"I'll never forget the day I stepped out of my bedroom just as all four of these girls went sailing down this very same banister together, giggling in delight thinking no one was watching. I felt bad about having to scold them, they were having such a good time; but I nearly had heart failure before they safely reached the bottom." She glanced at them and smiled. "It doesn't seem possible that you could now be grown, soon to be married and have babies of your own."

Nick placed two chairs next to the tree for them, and kissed Granny on the cheek before taking a seat on the floor. "We promise to take good care of them, Granny."

He wrapped his arm affectionately around Abby's shoulders as she moved from the piano bench and sat on the floor next to him. Nick glanced at Granny in time to see her smile when Matt, Jordan, and Greg nodded their heads in agreement with him.

Abby picked up her guitar and sang 'Silent Night' along with Michelle, Sandy, and Nicole. Their four-part harmony blended beautifully. Granny leaned over to Granddad and said just loud enough for Nick to hear. "It's good to see the girls back together and have Abigail playing her guitar once again." Baby Scotty started to fuss and Nick was pleased to see Abby gently take him from his sister Amy. Abby placed him over her shoulder and patted his diapered bottom until he went to sleep.

Michelle and Matt sat on the sofa eating popcorn, along with Sandy and Jordan. Nicole sat next to Greg checking out the presents under the tree. "Joy fills my heart, Audrey at the happiness our granddaughters have found in these wonderful young men. I can't begin to explain the thrill I feel at having them all here at home with us and on this special night to celebrate the birth of our Savior.

Granny took hold of Granddad's hand. "Look there across the room.

Our four sons and two grandsons are sitting in front of the television watching the football game. Our daughter-in-laws are at the table playing scrabble. They are decent men and women that we've raised together with the Lord's guidance to know his love." She smiled. "I'm just so thankful to have them all here."

******

Abby glanced over at her grandparents as her grandmother stood to get everyone's attention. "It's time to open gifts." She smiled. They didn't hesitate; everyone gathered and sat on the carpet around the Christmas tree as Granny sat back down in her chair.

"Jared." Granny called to her oldest grandson. "Would you do the honors of playing Santa please?"

"Sure Granny." Jared reached

underneath the tree and began handing out the gifts to each one.

After all the gifts had been handed out and opened, Granny glanced at Jared and smiled. "All right now, Dear. You can pass out the four gifts I told you about earlier."

Jared picked up four large packages from under the tree that were wrapped exactly alike, Abby noticed. Her oldest brother handed one to her, and one to each of his cousins, before taking his seat.

"Abigail, Michelle, Sandy, and Nicloe. I would like for each of you to open these gifts, then I have something I'd like to share with you."

The girls unwrapped the homemade quilts from their grandmother and shrieked in delight. Each one made in the same wedding ring pattern but in different colors, on an off white background. Abby's red, kelly green, and yellow, Michelle's, Navy, green, and yellow, Sandy's, navy, burgundy, and forest green, and Nicole's, rust, yellow, and orange.

Abby jumped up first and hugged her grandmother. "Granny, the quilt is beautiful. Thank you, it will look so pretty on a quilt stand in our new house."

Michelle laid her quilt down and followed with a hug of her own.

"Granny, thank you. The quilt is gorgeous; it will have a special place in my home."

Sandy, next in line hugged Granny. "Thank you for my quilt. I have always loved mom and dad's and I'm delighted to now have one of my own.

Nicole waited patiently for Sandy to sit down, then she hugged granny. "Thank you, for such a special gift. The colors are so bright, the quilt is beautiful and will look lovely on my bed."

After the girls were seated, Granny spoke again. "I started a tradition long ago, by making a quilt for each of my children on their first Christmas in their new home. Now I'm making one for each of my grandchildren. I'm very proud of each one of you. I know all four of you moved away due to problems in your lives. But you've resolved them and are doing very well. I'm proud of you." She looked at each one.

"I'd like at this time to welcome my soon to be grandson's, to the Forrester family." She smiled. "I'll look forward to making more quilts and more memories in the future. God has truly made something good out of all four situations. We are certainly blessed and I can't thank Him enough, for bringing you back home again."

Abby smiled as she heard Granny say to Granddaddy. "Wasn't it interesting to watch as each of our girls had a different reaction to my words. Abby smiled at Nick, Michelle took hold of Matt's hand, Sandy looked up at Jordan, and Nicole turned the ring on her finger as Greg whispered something in her ear. Each generation has brought its own blessings. I can hardly wait to see what the next one brings.

ABOUT THE AUTHOR

Jeanie Smith Cash lives in the country in Southwest Missouri, in the heart of the Ozarks, with her husband, Andy, her children, grandchildren and family, and she adores them all. She is a member of ACFW and has six books published. Jeanie gives her Lord and Savior the credit for her writing career and her loving family. She loves chocolate, collecting dolls, crocheting, spoiling her grandchildren, spending time with her family and traveling. Jeanie loves to read and write Christian Romance, and believes a salvation message inside of a good story, could possibly touch someone who wouldn't be reached in any other way. She loves to hear from her readers. You may contact her through her Email: jeaniesmithcash@yahoo.com and please feel free to join her Newsletter at: http://groups.yahoo.com/group/JeanieSmithCashsNewsletter Other books by this author are available at www.amazon.com

Made in the USA
Columbia, SC
08 September 2021